TIME HOP SWEETS SHOP

Cupcakes with Sally Ride

By Kyla Steinkraus
Illustrated by Katie Wood

www.rourkeeducationalmedia.com

Edited by: Keli Sipperley
Cover and Interior layout by: Kathy Walsh
Cover and Interior Illustrations by: Katie Wood

Library of Congress PCN Data

Cupcakes with Sally Ride / Kyla Steinkraus
(Time Hop Sweets Shop)
ISBN 978-1-68342-333-1 (hard cover)(alk. paper)
ISBN 978-1-68342-429-1 (soft cover)
ISBN 978-1-68342-499-4 (e-Book)
Library of Congress Control Number: 2017931180

Printed in the United States of America,
North Mankato, Minnesota

Dear Parents and Teachers,

Fiona and Finley are just like any modern-day kids. They help out with the family business, face struggles and triumphs at school, travel through time with important historical figures ...

Well, maybe that part's not so ordinary. At the Time Hop Sweets Shop, anything can happen, at any point in time. The family bakery draws customers from all over the map–and all over the history books. And when Tick Tock the parrot squawks, Fiona and Finley know an adventure is about to begin!

These beginner chapter books are designed to introduce students to important people in U.S. history, turning their accomplishments into adventures that Fiona, Finley, and young readers get to experience right along with them.

Perfect as read-alouds, read-alongs, or independent readers, books in the Time Hop Sweets Shop series were written to delight, inform, and engage your child or students by making each historical figure memorable and relatable. Each book includes a biography, comprehension questions, websites for further reading, and more.

We look forward to our time travels together!

Happy Reading,
Rourke Educational Media

Table of Contents

The Cupcake King

"Mmmm! This is yummy!" Fiona said. She stuck her finger in the frosting and licked it.

Her brother Finley pulled his cupcake away. "No fair. Stop eating my cupcakes! I need them for the bake sale." Finley's nickname was Cupcake King. He baked the best cupcakes in the whole world.

Finley and Fiona's mom and dad owned the Sweets Shop. It was a bakery with old-fashioned treats like molasses cookies, cider cake, and rhubarb tarts. After school, the kids helped make wonderful desserts.

Finley was a year older than Fiona, but Fiona was just as tall. She could do anything Finley could do. Almost. She couldn't make cupcakes as delicious as Finley could.

"It's not fair," Fiona said with a sigh. "I

"See you soon!" Tick Tock squawked.

The Big Launch!

The Sweets Shop began to spin. It felt like being inside a washing machine!

Fiona loved it.

Finley hated it. His face turned green.

"Wowza!" Fiona gasped.

The world stopped spinning. They were sitting inside the space shuttle. And they wore blue spacesuits, just like Sally.

"Buckle up," Sally said. "This is the *Challenger* space shuttle. It's thirty stories tall." She introduced the kids to the rest of the crew. "This is Norman, Robert, Frederick, and John."

The men waved and said hello.

Sally closed the visor on their helmets. Fiona and Finley breathed through the oxygen supply in their spacesuits. "Ready for outer space?" she asked.

Finley's heart pounded in his chest. Fiona could barely breathe. Ten seconds before liftoff, the countdown began. "Ten, nine, eight, seven . . ."

"Three, two, one," Fiona said excitedly.

The rockets lit. A loud rumbling roar filled the shuttle. The sound was deafening! The shuttle launched into the air. It went faster and faster. Fiona and Finley's heads rattled inside their helmets. The engines and the rockets thundered in their ears. It was so loud, Finley had to turn down his hearing aid.

Finley swallowed. *Was everything working properly? What if something went wrong?* Finley thought.

Up, up, and up they went. They flew past the clouds.

"I can't move!" Fiona shouted.

Sally laughed. "The force of 3 G's, three times the force of the gravity we feel on Earth, is pushing us back against our seats. It will be over soon."

After two rumbling, roaring minutes, it suddenly became quiet and smooth. "What happened?" Finley asked.

"The rocket boosters are empty. They broke away from the shuttle. They'll glide back to Earth with parachutes."

"But not us," Finley breathed. "We're not going back to Earth."

Eight minutes after the shuttle launch, the engines cut off. The force was gone. Sally's book and pencils floated in midair. All gravity was gone, even the normal gravity from Earth!

"We're in orbit now," Sally said. "One hundred and sixty miles above the Earth."

Floating in Outer Space

Fiona and Finley unstrapped their seatbelts. They floated, too! Fiona drifted around the cabin, bumping into the walls. Finley sat on the ceiling. He laughed so hard, he had to hold his stomach.

Fiona looked out the windows and gasped. Earth was a huge, spinning ball beneath them. The oceans were a beautiful blue, the deserts bright orange. They could see mountains and canyons and whole oceans. A beautiful sunrise rose over the edge of the planet.

"I'm hungry!" Finley said. "Wait, how do we eat?"

Sally handed them each a squishy pouch and a spoon. Fiona opened it up and tasted it. "Not too bad."

"We eat all our meals this way. Our food has to be sticky or it will float away!"

Fiona laughed. It was funny to think about escaping food.

Finley shook his head. "No cupcakes in space. How sad."

"What about sleeping?" Fiona asked.

"We can anchor our feet, attach ourselves to the wall, or sleep floating."

"Wowza," Fiona whispered. "I wish I could float-sleep at home!"

"What about brushing your teeth?"

"We use toothpaste that we don't spit out," Sally said. "That would be gross, huh?"

Fiona made a face. "It's a good thing NASA thinks about this stuff ahead of time."

Finley floated over to the window. "Didn't the sun just rise a little while ago?"

Sally grinned. "We'll get to see a sunrise and a sunset every ninety minutes for the next six days, two hours, and twenty-four minutes that we're in space."

Fiona pushed off the wall with her feet. It felt like flying! "How did you become an astronaut?"

"One day I saw a notice in the newspaper from NASA. They wanted people to become astronauts. I applied that very day!"

"Was it hard?" Finley asked.

"Oh, yes. I took many tests. Out of eight thousand people, I was one of thirty-five chosen. Once I was picked, I went through a year of training. I learned to fly a jet and jump with a parachute. I learned all about how the space shuttle worked."

"Wowza," Fiona said.

"Do you just float around all day?" Finley crossed his legs in the air. He could get used to this!

"I'm the flight engineer and a mission specialist. We have many jobs. We'll release satellites. We'll conduct experiments in

space. We'll study how gravity affects the behavior of carpenter ants. And we'll research how plants grow without gravity."

"So, you're a scientist and an astronaut?" Finley asked.

"Yep."

"See, Finley?" Fiona stuck out her tongue. "Girls can be the best, too."

Finley tapped his hearing aid. "I can't hear you."

"Yes, you can. Don't make me float over there!"

Finley laughed. "Okay, you're right. I'm sorry for what I said, Fiona. You can be the best astronaut. But . . ."

"But what?" Fiona asked.

"I'm going to be the best baker in space! Outer space needs the Cupcake King!"

Sally Ride rubbed her stomach. "Speaking of cupcakes, let's go back to the Sweets Shop. I really want to try one of your famous cupcakes, Finley."

As everything began to spin and shake, Fiona looked at planet Earth one last time. It was beautiful. "See you soon," she whispered.

About Sally Ride

Sally Ride was born on May 26, 1956 in Encino, California. Her parents raised her to study hard and do her best. Sally loved to read, play sports, and learn about science. She also loved outer space. In college, she majored in physics and competed in tennis tournaments. In 1978, she earned her Ph.D. When she read a notice from NASA in her college newspaper, she applied to become an astronaut. After many tests, interviews, and training, she became an astronaut in 1979.

On June 18, 1983, at 7:33 a.m., Sally Ride became the first American woman to enter space on the *Challenger*. During the six days in space, the *Challenger* orbited Earth 97 times. When they returned, Sally refused any interviews that didn't include her entire crew. On October 5, 1984, Sally Ride launched into space one more time. They launched a satellite that would help scientists predict long-range weather forecasts. After leaving NASA, Sally became a physics professor in San Diego, California. She is also the director of the California Space Institute.

Q and A with Kyla Steinkraus

What do you love most about writing?

I love that I get to discover all kinds of new things I didn't know before. For this book, I researched outer space. I learned what it takes to become an astronaut. I'm always learning new things.

Did you ever want to be an astronaut?

I think astronauts are amazing, but I like keeping my feet on planet Earth! It would be really fun to experience space for a week. Like a space vacation!

What is your favorite thing about space?

Like Fiona, I would love to try float-sleeping! Or just floating around in general. I would pretend I was flying everywhere I went.

Comprehension Questions

1.) Why was Fiona mad at Finley?

2.) Name three fun things you learned about astronauts and space.

3.) What were a few of Sally Ride's jobs while she was in space?

Websites to Visit

www.ducksters.com/biography/women_leaders/sally_ride.php

www.nasa.gov/audience/forstudents/k-4/stories/nasa-knows/who-was-sally-ride-k4.html

www.timeforkids.com/news/chat-sally-ride/10901

Writing Prompt

Imagine you are on the space shuttle *Challenger* in outer space. What would your day be like? What would you do? How would you sleep? What would you eat? Write a paragraph about the perfect day in outer space.

About the Author

Kyla Steinkraus lives in Atlanta, Georgia with her husband, two kids, and two spoiled cats. She is the author of more than 30 kids' books. She loves writing and learning about new things. If she could go to outer space, she would want to visit Mars and the moon. When she's not writing, she enjoys board games, hiking, reading, and drawing.